TRIUMPHANT
WOMEN

TRIUMPHANT
WOMEN

STORIES OF COURAGE

VOLUME ONE

Lori Wieters, Ph.D.
Calli Wieters, Life Coach

Claim your significance!
Lori Wieters

Be Triumphant!
Calli W

TABLE OF CONTENTS

TRIUMPHANT WOMEN:
Stories of Courage

Our Stories

TRIUMPHANT WOMEN:
Stories of Courage

Lori Wieters, Ph.D.

FOREWORD

In January of 2009, I sat in front of my computer setting my goals for the year. One that bubbled to the top of the list was my goal of publishing a book. Since I had received my Ph.D. in Organization and Management in June of 2007, my goal had been to publish on a regular basis. Due to a whole series of excuses, I had failed to realize this goal. I believe the biggest excuse was fear – possibly even fear of success.

As I sat there and stared at this goal again, I thought, "It is time!" The next question that came to mind was, "What do I publish?" I could write a leadership or business related book. That idea came and went quickly. There was no passion in it. "Or, do I feed my passion for helping women?"

I have been volunteering for several years to help disadvantaged women through life coaching, career development and personal development. The excitement I felt at the thought of writing a book about women who have overcome tremendous odds to become who they are today indicated to me that I was on the right track. I decided to call the book *Triumphant Women: Stories of Courage*.

As I developed this idea further and began to research the world of publishing, I knew I wanted to write a book similar to the *Chicken Soup for the Soul* series. I began to pitch my idea to family and friends and they got excited. They all had a story to tell. On January 4th, 2009, I sent out an email to all my family and friends asking them for submissions, promising them only copies of the book in return. I also asked them to forward the request on to people they knew that had a story to tell.

In March 2009, Calli, my daughter-in-law, came on board as my partner in this project. She is an unbelievably talented woman and I am honored that she wanted to work with me and with all of you. As I started receiving submissions, I cried through every one for a lot of reasons – first, I could not believe what some of these women had gone through in their lives to become the people I know today; second, the fact that they were willing to relive the experience through writing about it; and, finally, the awe inspiring idea that they wanted to share their lives with me and the rest of the world. Unbelievable!

When the thought of authoring the book become reality, I thought I could get away with just being the author – no one needed to know my story. That thought quickly dissipated. To be credible, I would have to be just as vulnerable and tell my story, too. Before I do that, I would like to introduce you to one of the philosophies I live my life by. I have never been overtly religious but I am a Christian and believe in a powerful God. Anytime I thought that life could not get worse, I received this message from a trusted friend or pastor – "God will NEVER give you anything YOU can't handle."

That statement was usually followed by something like, "Fortunately or unfortunately, you are going through this so you are able to help someone else. Look for something good in this and/ or what life lesson you are supposed to pass on during your lifetime."

When I received this message, this was the last thing I wanted to hear; however, today, this is how I live my life. Therefore, I want to share my story with you. This is just an example of the women you will find in this book. As you read, I hope that you will be able to relate your triumphant story to my story or one of the other beautiful women represented through their stories. Triumphant women are all around us!

ACKNOWLEDGEMENTS

A heartfelt thank you to all the amazing people we were surrounded by during this project. These people were willing to help us with this project, on their own time, and it means the world to us!

Therefore, we would like to help them with their business ventures by telling you about them. If you need any of their services, please feel free to contact them directly. They are all amazing individuals, without whom we would not have this book to share with you all today.

A loving "thank you" goes to the women who were willing to let other women peek into their lives. These women are amazing examples of what it truly means to be a Triumphant Women. As our editor commented, "Reading these stories was like peeking in someone's window and not being able to turn away; it was uncomfortable but not uncomfortable enough to stop reading." We want to thank you for sharing yourself with the world! Be sure to visit the website to see what these triumphant women are up to today.

Our logo work was created by "JT" Thurston of Graphic Design in Phoenix, Arizona. He was very patient with us as we perfected the look of our logo. We want to thank him for his services on this project. If you like the look of our logo, please feel free to contact him at *www.graphicdesignphx.com*.

A special thanks to our webmaster/creator, Robert McCorkle. Words cannot express our gratitude to you as you walked us through the process of building our website. Although you were pressed for time, you gave us your time and ideas freely. You were both innovative and creative throughout the process. We know we had a big wish list and somehow you made it all work. We wish you the best as you start your life in a new state with your family. If you like the look and feel of our website, Robert is available for website projects. Please contact him at *www.RAinsites.com.*

We want to extend an additional thank you to our photographer, Kellie Gilliss, of The Big Picture Fine Art & Photography, and to our publishing team at Serey/Jones Publishers. Thank you for your time and your creativity. We love the work that you have done for us. We couldn't have done this without your expertise.

To the love of our lives, our husbands, Steve and Steven, thank you for helping out with the little ones while we worked to put the website and the book together and for all the support and encouragement. We love you both and could not have put this project together without you. To our family and friends, you too, have played and will play an integral part in the success of this project.

We are all Triumphant!

Lori and Calli

TRIUMPHANT
WOMEN

Lori

Part 1 and Part II

Many people know me as a mother, a grandmother, a daughter, a professor, a coach, a mentor, an employee, a manager or a leader. Very few people really know me, what makes me tick or what drives me to be who I am. I have been able to hide Lori for many years. To think about writing about her is kind of scary. I tend to think about the former Lori in third person. Through some purposeful reflection, decision-making and divine intervention, that Lori is not a reflection of who I am today. I do not dwell on that person but appreciate the role she played in my life. This purposeful segmentation (thus, Part 1 and a Part 2) of my life is probably why telling this story is so hard. I am just very thankful I had an opportunity to have a Part 2.

Part 1

I am going to censor this part of my life because my mother is still alive and I assume she will want to read this book. Although I blamed her for many years, she has to know that I forgive her for what I am about to write. As an adult having similar experiences, I now understand what she was going through.

Let me start by setting the stage. My brother was born in 1960 and I was born in 1962 in Indiana. Things were not going well between my mom and dad, and when I was only three months old, they divorced. After the divorce, we relocated to Arizona to live with my grandma and grandpa. My mom eventually rented a little house and we started our lives as a small family. I enjoyed school and our family time. One of my favorite memories is of the times we went to the drive-in movies together. We would pack popcorn and fruit juice and spend the evening in the car watching movies. It was an inexpensive way to have fun. Eventually, my mom qualified for a home through a single-mother program and we moved to our own home. What an exciting time! I had my own room and a lot of neighborhood friends. We were on the right track.

When I was about 10 or 11 years old, the fun family life as we knew it stopped suddenly. My mom met and married a man I refer to as the "spawn of the devil." I am not sure whether or not she would appreciate the nickname, but I am sure that today she would agree with the term. For many years, my brother and I lived with the physical and mental abuse this man dished out. At one point, I ran away from home to get away from it and was gone for several days – living in one of my friend's rooms (until her mom found me). I was returned to the horror we called a family life. I tried to tell people what was going on and no one believed me. I was called a liar and labeled as incorrigible. My mom was blind to the situation and seemed to support it. I kept asking myself, "Doesn't she see what is going on?"

In addition to the abuse, both my mom and step-dad drank a lot. What had started out as a wonderful childhood experience turned into an abusive, alcohol-driven existence where my brother and I became the punching bags.

I believe that to hide all that was going on in our family, my mother and step-dad moved us to a small town in the middle of no-where Illinois. This was the place where "the spawn's" family lived. When we moved, I no longer had a support system. School was a weird place. I was in junior high and had just been transported back in time. The educational system wasn't as advanced as it was in the Phoenix area. I made friends easily but was so embarrassed about my living situation that I did not want to invite them to my home. We lived in a series of old farm houses outside of town. Many of the houses did not have running water or indoor plumbing. The physical and mental abuse and the alcohol consumption became a normal part of our existence.

I started sneaking beer when I was 13 or 14. My mom and step-dad never noticed. It became easier and easier to steal and drink. It made me forget what a horrible place my home was. My mom and step-dad were members of a small town band and played gigs on other farms where a keg of beer would be open for consumption. I, along with many of the other kids, would sneak drinks of the beer. Drinking beer became a part of many weekend pleasures. They never noticed my drinking because they were drunk a lot of the time themselves. Looking back, my only godsend was that I loved sports. During the week, my escape was being an athlete. I could leave early in the morning on the bus to go to school and come back on the players' bus at about dinner time. On game nights I wasn't home until late. When I got home I could lock myself in my room and do "homework." I didn't have to see what was going on in the house.

Sports were something I discovered that I did very well. During my high school years, I participated in four: softball, volleyball, basketball, and track. One of the kudos I would like to give my mom here is that she supported every sport I played and came out to as many of the home games as she could. This was when I felt the closest to her – and didn't feel like the liar that I had been labeled early on.

Weekends, especially after I started driving, became one big party. I had progressed from just alcohol to alcohol and a little pot here and there. I think mom suspected something but never confronted me until after I graduated from high school. I can remember the conversation as if it happened yesterday. I was playing softball in a summer league between my high school graduation and leaving for college. The game got rained out. At the tender age of 17, I went to the bar with my team members and got served (many times). We then hit an 'after hour' bar and, consequently, I strolled in at around 5:00 a.m. My mom opened the door as I walked up to it and asked, "Are you drunk?"

I said, "Yes" and went to my room to sleep it off. We had

quite a talk when I woke up. It went something like, "How can I trust you to go to college and do what you need to do when you do this kind of thing here?"

I wanted to scream at her to wake up! I had been doing this 'kind of thing' for many years and it was getting out of control. Instead, I assured her that this was a one time thing and that she had nothing to worry about.

My love for sports led me to a full-ride scholarship at a university in Iowa. I was finally going to be able to leave home and start anew. I was really excited that I was going to school where no one knew me, where I could build my own life. Off to college I went to escape, not understanding what a rare opportunity I had been given.

I spent four years at the university, playing three sports (softball, volleyball and basketball) in the beginning and then eventually settling into volleyball and basketball during my junior and senior years. The weekends were still spent at parties where everyone ended up drunk. I was lucky that the school part was easy for me. I found that if I attended class and did the work that I could pass all the classes. No one had ever labeled me as "smart" so I thought school was easy for everyone. I didn't appreciate this until many years later. I never went "home" after my freshman/sophomore summer. I always found ways to support myself through the breaks and summers. I still had a lot of anger to deal with and it was just easier not to go backward. Reflecting on my college experience, it is a wonder that I was able to juggle everything – school, work, sports, a work-study job, sorority functions, a demanding boyfriend, and parties. I graduated in 1983 with a Bachelor of Science degree in Education with a 3.58 grade point average. Today, I wonder how successful I would have been if I had understood the value of this gift at the time.

Within a few days after graduation, I stopped by to see my mom at her home to switch out cars so I could relocate to Arizona. While I was away at college, she finally "woke up" and divorced "the spawn" and had remarried a kind and thoughtful man. They were busy building a new life together. I wanted to return to Phoenix and my family.

Thirty hours later, I showed up on my aunt's and uncle's doorstep with my only possessions – a car, a few clothes, and a couple of boxes of trophies and pictures. Up to that point, that was all, my life had amounted to. My aunt and uncle had always played a mother/father role in my life and I felt like I was finally home. It had been a long journey.

Unfortunately, I had one more lesson to learn before I could really enter Part 2 of my life. Shortly after arriving in Phoenix, I was working and enjoying my new life. Then I met a man who would become my first husband. The man fit into my previous life style of parties and fun. Although I vowed to make a new start in Phoenix, I slipped into old habits. The drinking started again and, now that I was 21, I could get into bars. This made drinking more accessible. We had such a blast together that we decided to start a new life together. We rented an apartment and lived together for almost a year (much to the horror of my family) before we got married. Not quite a year later, I found out that I was pregnant. All of a sudden our world as we knew it blew up in our faces. I had our daughter in June of 1986 and in January of 1987 we separated after he announced that he decided he did not want to be a husband or a father. It came down to the fact that I was not able to take care of him any more. I was devastated. All of a sudden I was my mother. I was a single mother with a six-month old baby. We lost our house and I moved back in to live at my aunt's and uncle's house. Despite the "I told you so-s", I was always thankful that they were there for me.

They helped me take care of my daughter while I worked and tried to pull my life together. During this period of time, I lost 40 pounds in a span of three months and my employer sent me to counseling to stop the downward spiral I appeared to be on. Through this period, I became strong again by identifying a new sense of purpose. I had to be a role model for my daughter. I was re-energized. I wanted her to grow to be a strong, confident woman. The only way I knew to be that role model was to personally achieve great things that she could be proud of and possibly emulate in her life. I never wanted her to hate or blame me for being too weak or afraid to tackle the tough situations in life.

As a part of ending Part 1 of my life, my counselor wanted me to go through the process of setting goals for the next man I wanted in our life. This was an attempt to prevent me from falling into another alcoholic and/or possibly abusive relationship. She told me to read a book titled "Women Who Love Too Much" by Robin Norwood, which gave me a great perspective on why I had chosen my ex-husband. My goals centered on the stability that doesn't come with alcoholic tendencies and went something like this:

The man I want:

- Owns his house and is not asking to move in with me.
- Has been employed in his job for at least five years.
- Does not drink or smoke.
- Enjoys sports.
- Is handsome, romantic and loving.
- Loves me for who I am and doesn't want me to change.
- Has children, as I am coming to the marriage with one child (would prefer if he has a daughter as a way to ensure that he doesn't abuse children).
- Has the ability to love a child that is not his own.
- Is a family man in that his world centers on the value of "family."
- Is fun to be with and smart.

I thought that the list was not achievable. I did not know it at the time but I had set my first real stretch goal. There was some sense of security in thinking that I had set the goal so high that a man would never measure up to this list. I refused to settle for less than a check mark in every box. Finally, I was safe from feeling like I had to be in a relationship and would concentrate on taking care of my daughter all by myself.

Part 2

Those who believe that there is a higher power playing in our lives may agree with me that God has a sense of humor. I am sure he said something like, "My child, I see this list you made for a man. For all your suffering, your hard work and renewed sense of purpose, I have just the man for you and your daughter. "

Enter the love of my life, Steve. I met Steve in August of 1987, after I had sworn off men in my life, and began checking things off my list. He had owned his house for several years, had a job for many years, and had been in the Navy previous to that. He did not drink or smoke, enjoyed playing and watching sports, and had been an athlete his entire life. He was (and still is) so attractive, romantic and loving, allowed me to be me (and still doesn't ask me to change), had custody of two children who were living with him – a boy (7) and a girl (9) – loved other children as evidenced by his relationships with his nieces and nephews, centered his world around his family and, as a bonus, was fun to be with and smart.

I wanted to run. I surely wasn't worthy of checking all the boxes off. This was too good to be true. I can tell you now that it <u>was</u> too good to be true. The perfect excuse to run surfaced shortly after I met him. He admitted to me that his ex-wife was living in the house with him.

He claimed it was nothing and knew he should have ended it a long time ago but it was convenient and his children liked her being there. I told him that I would not be the "other woman" in any relationship. I wasn't very nice about it and called him several very descriptive names. The hurt in his eyes led me to do one smart thing. I left the door open. I said that if he ever found himself single, we could continue to explore what a relationship might look like between us.

After this conversation, I was actually very relieved and didn't think I would ever hear from him again. We had the initial conversation on a Saturday night and I received a call the following Wednesday that he was single and that his ex-wife had moved out. He wanted me and my daughter to meet his children the following Saturday. We were married four months later. Many people said it would never last.

Fast forward, 22 years. Reflecting on the experience is very rewarding. It was not easy bringing two families together into one but somehow we did it by dedicating our efforts to being a cohesive family. The children (now adults) look at each other as brother and sisters, not as step-siblings. All three of our children are successful in their careers and are constantly striving for new achievements. It has been fun watching them grow and develop into who they are today. Watching them create their own families validates all of our effort. In the last three years, we have been blessed with three grandchildren. It has been exciting for both Steve and me to be role models for them. We have persevered through all the muck and mire that life brought us and have created a marriage centered on family values and love. I had successfully replaced the void that alcohol had filled with love.

From a personal perspective, I could not have asked for a more loving and supportive life partner. Throughout our marriage, Steve has allowed me to achieve my own goals. In 1997, I went back to school to get my Masters of Business Administration in Management and received my degree in 1999. Shortly after that, I went back to school to get my Ph.D. The Ph.D. was the ultimate goal that would offer the credibility for me to write books and speak to thousands (my life goal). Steve was there every step of the way – from listening to me cry about how hard it was, to reading my dissertation; he received an honorary Ph.D. from me when I graduated.

Today, I coach and train others to be more effective in their personal and professional lives and I absolutely love it. I am in what some people term as the "sweet spot" in life. I have a rewarding career, a loving husband and family, and am looking forward to many more situations I can triumph through.

Final Thoughts:

For me, the difference between Part I and Part II of life are three basic elements. First, you have to be willing to find out who you are and not let what has happened *to* you determine your future. Second, identify what you want in life through purposeful exploration of your talents, uniqueness, and desires and then set appropriate life goals. Finally, admit that you are significant and that you have a lot to give this world.

Remember, *"God* will NEVER give you anything YOU can't handle."

Now I am going to say it to you, "Fortunately or unfortunately, you are going through this so you are able to help someone else. Look for something good in this and/or what life lesson you are supposed to pass on during your lifetime."

You are a Triumphant Woman!

TRIUMPHANT
WOMEN

Calli

Baby, It Will Be Okay

It was January 7th, 2009 and I was heading to the hospital early that morning to be induced to deliver my son. I never thought the day would arrive. I had so many reservations this time around. As we were driving, I reflected on the past few years. Three years prior I delivered my beautiful, fiery red headed girl who was born ready to compete with the world. My pregnancy was so easy. I was never sick, and had no complications. I never imagined what the road ahead of me would have in store when my husband and I found out we were pregnant for the second time.

October of 2007, I found out I was pregnant. We were so excited to have another baby and continue to grow our family. At first, everything seemed to be as normal as it was with my daughter. Although I was a little more tired than the first time and felt different pains in my body, I thought it was because it was my second baby and that my body was just changing. Overall, I felt well. We had check-ups with the doctor every three weeks and everything was progressing normally.

At the 10-week mark, I was scheduled to go in and hear the heartbeat for the first time. I remember lying waiting to hear that beautiful sound. I think that's when, as a mom, you really feel something amazing is happening and that you have a hand in a gift from God. My husband had the little recorder out – ready to record the first heartbeat (something that we would have on a little cassette to hear forever). The doctor seemed to be having trouble hearing the heartbeat. I was not worried as she moved the disc around my belly. My daughter's heartbeat was difficult to find as well. After a few minutes, no one in the room was talking anymore. The doctor asked me to get up and move to another room where she had a small ultrasound machine. We moved into the room and as I lay down, she began to do an ultrasound on me. The machine was very small, and she said she was just having a hard time seeing or hearing anything. So she scheduled us for another ultrasound the next morning.

The next morning we got up early and headed out for our ultrasound appointment. We got to the office and the tech called us back. At this point, I did not know I was about to lie down and have my world crash around me. I did not believe that there was going to be anything wrong. How could there be? I had a baby already with no complications whatsoever.

The technician began the procedure and didn't say anything. If I had I known what I was in for, I never would have looked up at that ultrasound screen. After lying there for a few minutes while the tech did the procedure, I realized I did not hear anything. I looked at the screen and it was completely black. There was a shape of a baby but there was nothing flickering in the chest. This was nothing like anything I had experienced in my prior ultrasounds. Maybe I was still in denial at this point and, of course, the technician could not discuss what they discovered. While I was in the restroom, after the procedure, my husband asked the technician "Is there something wrong?"

All she could say was that our doctor would call us. I went about my day worried and unsure about what the doctor was going to call and tell me. I just spent a lot of time lying down on the couch with my husband rubbing my head. I know, deep down, we both knew what was happening, but we did not say anything to each other.

Finally, that afternoon, my doctor called and I had my husband answer it. I heard what she was telling him and tried to keep myself collected. The doctor asked my husband to hand the phone to me so she could discuss what was going on. I will never forget her words. "I am sorry, Calli, the fetus did not survive."

I cried as she talked to me about the rest of the process and what my options were. As I hung up the phone, I remember the emptiness and sadness I had for a baby that should have been. My husband was so strong for me. I never saw him cry, but he let me know how sad he was, and he reassured me that we would be okay. In his private times, I would hear him crying and it broke my heart. "How could this have happened?" I would ask myself. "I had already delivered a very healthy baby and nothing went wrong with her!"

The next morning I was scheduled to go into the hospital and have a procedure to extract the baby. I went into the hospital very sad but I knew I needed to get it done to move on. I waved to my husband, my dad, and friends as I was wheeled back for my procedure. The next thing I knew, I woke up in recovery. I was crying a lot and the nurse leaned over and said, "Why are you crying, honey? Are you sad about the baby?"

I nodded my head and she told me it would be okay. I was allowed to go home that night. It was strange to think that I wasn't pregnant anymore and I didn't even have a baby to show for it. I was only ten weeks along, but a mother's love is instant. You don't have to see your child to know it is your gift from God and that it is a part of you.

This all happened a couple days before Christmas 2007. I will never forget not wanting to be around all the family who I felt would be looking at me and feeling bad for me. It's difficult, in a time like this, to say if you really want attention or not. If someone does tell you that they are sorry for your loss, you cry; and if someone doesn't ask, you think they don't care and you cry. The whole experience was very emotional – and still is, and will always be.

As time has passed, I have learned that everything will be okay and it just wasn't that precious little angel's time to be here. I know to this day that the only reason I am okay is because I had a very vivid dream one night. God was holding the tiniest little baby and he said to me, "Everything's all right; I have him."

I remember waking up smiling and knowing that, yes, everything **would** be all right.

I was so afraid to try again, but I knew if I put my faith in God he would take care of us. I found out I was pregnant once more in April 2008. We wanted to be so excited, but due to problems with the last time, I think everyone held back their excitement. We were all afraid it could happen again. So I did everything the doctor told me to make sure this little one would arrive on time.

At about 28 weeks, they did a very in-depth ultrasound. I was afraid to lose another baby. With our heads high, my husband and I went into the ultrasound office, expecting that surely this time everything would be just fine.

As the technician moved the instrument all over my stomach, she kept going back to the baby's head but never said a word. I left there thinking everything went perfectly only to have my doctor tell me at my next check up that they had found a cyst on the baby's brain.

I held back tears until I left her office. My husband just kept saying it would be okay. I was scheduled for another ultrasound several weeks later when the doctor would tell us whether the cyst had grown or had dissolved. We prayed it would be gone.

That day of the ultrasound finally came. As the procedure was being done, the tech passed over the baby's head, and said, "The cyst is gone. It has dissolved."

We were thrilled!

The rest of the pregnancy went great and soon we were driving to the hospital for our baby's birth. Our beautiful baby boy arrived in the afternoon of January 7, 2009. I couldn't believe it. It had been such a long road.

Today it amazes me at how this journey has changed me. Although I am young, I know that we women are strong and deal with so much heartache in life – yet we survive. With faith and a positive perspective, we can accomplish the most amazing things.

Through this experience, I have learned that things happen in their own time and that going through struggles in life only makes us stronger and more prepared to tackle future obstacles. We are amazing! We deal with caring for the sick in our families, losing loved ones, caring for our children, and making sure our family has dinner and are clean and ready for the world. We are the glue that holds our families together and we can triumph over anything! We are triumphant women!

TRIUMPHANT
WOMEN

Gloria

Healing through Poetry

I was a woman of 40, married for 22 years, with two teenagers. I had just received an Applied Science degree in office management and was recovering from being mauled by two very large dogs, when I was thrust into the world of divorce. After three weeks of non-stop crying, literally pulling the hair out of my head and watching my kids think only of their father, I decided I needed to work on myself. I entered into months of divorce therapy, attending many divorce networking groups, and then my kids moved out of the house to be with their traveling Super Dad. When I had to empty the house by having garage sales, get a moving van, and sell the house with no help, I decided to move out of state in order to start to heal.

My last winter before leaving, I shoveled a record 75 inches of snow, with no help. I guess I should mention that I am four feet eight inches, and weighed 92 pounds dripping wet. The snow piled up to six feet and I had to lift the shovel and throw it two feet over my head. The kids were told they didn't have to help me. I was totally and completely on my own. Of course the snow plows came along and I would have to start all over again.

My final wake-up call was watching my ex, who was an alcoholic and a diagnosed pathological liar, having a major mid-life crisis and cheating on me, all at the same time. He came several times a week to pick up our daughter and gave our son the van to drive around town. Both kids wanted to be with their dad because "he was more fun and took them places."

One day I just snapped and picked up a butcher knife as he pulled up to the house. I was absolutely shocked at myself. I put down the knife when I said to myself, while looking at my husband, you are **not** worth it. I will not ruin my life by stabbing you with a butcher knife.

From that moment on, I stopped pulling my hair out and went to the farthest room of the house so I wouldn't see my ex, hear him or talk to him every time he came over. I learned to hang up the phone when he called and verbally beat me up. While I thought it was rude to hang up the phone (that's what I had been taught), I learned to do it with a great feeling of control over who said what to me. It was very, very powerful.

I finally made up my mind to stop beating myself up and blaming myself for everything, and started to "wash that man right out of my hair." I wanted to be a very strong, independent woman. I wanted to heal and find out who I was and how strong I really was.

I watched women in the divorce groups, who were still pining for their exes. My psychologist asked me "when are you going to stop crying?" and "what do you want from this therapy?"

My answer –"to learn to live without a man!" I wanted to be strong, happy on my own, support myself, learn about who I was, what I did wrong, and how I could change that so I didn't repeat the past as I went along with my new life.

After the divorce, selling the house – and with my kids having turned against me with the help of their Super Dad – I decided to move to Arizona. Moving to Arizona was the best thing I could have done. My mom and a friend from one of the divorce groups were there.

I got a good job, rented an apartment and started to learn who I really was, inside and out. I started the healing process, started to grow, and found out I had a good work ethic. I was relaxing, making new friends, and having fun when I looked into getting my bachelor's degree from the University of Phoenix. I discovered that I was not dumb and stupid. I am so proud of earning that degree at 50, because it represents and validates that I do have a good mind. To me it is more than just a degree. It represents that I am still growing and learning, and loving it.

I began writing poetry in 1983. I started to grow one step at a time, and went two steps backwards for quite awhile. Although I had never written poetry before, never completed a class in poetry, and never learned what the rules of poetry were – one day I was just flooded with words. It didn't matter if I was driving or at a stop light, or on my break at work, the words just kept flowing and I just kept writing. On many occasions, I wrote until midnight. I kept paper and pencil in the car, by my bed at night, in the lunch room at work – it didn't matter. It took me almost three years of constant writing before I could begin to see that I was making strides in the growing department. I even lost my poems in a move at one time, only to find them again many years later and decided to put them in a scrapbook. That is another talent I found recently – scrapbooking my poems. You will see by my poetry how I started to grow.

I saw so many women in the various divorce groups going to therapy and two years later still stuck and suffering. I was asked, "What do you want out of therapy?" My answer – I want to learn how to live without a man, not to be suffering two years later. I attended several divorce network groups, continued therapy and I put the following letters on individual sheets of typing paper – I WILL SURVIVE – on my bedroom ceiling and repeated it every morning and every night before I went to sleep.

I WILL SURVIVE

I will survive your comforting love,
I will survive like a mourning dove.

I will survive your destructive lies,
I will survive your empty eyes.

I will survive the sleepless nights,
I will survive and soar to new heights.

I will survive the lonely days,
I will survive in many ways.

I will survive to blossom anew,
I will survive, I will survive!

If you have children, you then add something else in the mix that can be more difficult than going through a divorce. How are the kids reacting to the change of events? Have their personalities changed? Do you see behavioral changes? Are they taking sides? Do you see changes happening at school? Do they need a therapist just for them, to help keep them on track and to deal with any problems that might arise?

I felt these questions were extremely important; however, Super Dad said "there were no problems at all."

My son approached me one day (after he left home) and told me I needed to start going to the bars instead of sitting home. He also asked if I was changing the name I had used for 22 years. My daughter missed Super Dad so much that she was rarely home. When she wanted to go live with him, he didn't want her. I just said, "Deal with it."

You made the mess – now clean it up.

There are many mothers who wait like I did. Some are more fortunate than I was because they didn't have Super Dads who misrepresent everything that is said and leave you waiting in the terminal, wondering if someone is actually coming to see you or were they talked into another "vacation" that was more fun. You then drive back home alone and go into another downward spiral.

WE ARE THE MOTHERS WHO WAIT

We are the mothers, who gave you your lives,
For the children we want more than to survive.

We care, we love and try to provide,
For the children who end up taking sides.

We are the mothers, who are left alone,
Our children chose to go, they don't even phone.

We struggle through life with no assistance,
We call on inner strength to carry us the distance.

Our love is not measured by the care we give,
Only in ways we cannot live.

We are the mothers, who show much love,
Only a few who don't look down on us from above.

We wait for a letter or maybe a card,
Even these are censured by an unseen guard.

We are the mothers, who carry much pain,
For the children we hope to see once again.

We wait for a visit to be granted to us,
Then see how we're deceived and try not to fuss.

The date was set, the plane due in,
We never know until your luggage comes in.

We are the mothers, who cry silently,
As we wait for our passengers anxiously.

Our pain is not visible for the children to see,
We are the mothers, who just wait patiently.

When we see you are cheated mile after mile,
We are the mothers, who put on a smile.

Of our children who blindly try to carry it all,
We are the mothers, who wait for the fall.

We are the mothers, whose ties we'll not sever,
We are the mothers, who will love you forever.

He told me I would thank him one day because he left me. After a move out of state, a very good job offer, loss of weight, making new friends, and a new life for myself, I sent him this Thank You.

THANK YOU FOR FINDING SOMEONE ELSE

Thank you for the loving times we shared together,
For the fun of boating, skiing, camping and walking hand in hand.

Thank you for the plays, art shows, trips and beautiful red roses.

THANK YOU FOR FINDING SOMEONE ELSE

Thank you for giving me two beautiful children,
For the special times when you were kind, considerate and loving.

Thank you for knowing that I would be stronger without you,
For telling me that I would thank you one day.

THANK YOU FOR FINDING SOMEONE ELSE

Thank you for giving me the opportunity of knowing my own strengths,
For getting to know myself and who I really am.

Thank you for the chance to know what peace of mind really is.

THANK YOU FOR FINDING SOMEONE ELSE

Thank you for telling me I would thank you one day,
Today is that day. Thank you.

What a wonderful moment in time. This is one of my favorites. I was still was having ups and downs but they were farther and farther apart. I hope you will feel this way one of these days. Keep on keepin' on and you will get there. You will see the beautiful butterflies and marvel at their "specialness." You will see how special you are that day.

FREE

I'm as free as my beautiful butterflies,
To soar, to roam and look to the skies.

They are gentle and mellow with so much grace,
They're in no hurry, they're not in a race.

They float through the air with style and ease,
They go through life like a gentle breeze.

They are multicolor like crayons in a box,
Scattering about like seeds of lacy phlox.

How long do they live in a warm cocoon,
Before they break out to fully bloom.

To share their splendor for all about,
To glide through the flowers in and out.

They give much pleasure for the eye to see,
Like a camera who captures a single posey.

They come and go soaring high and low,
I also choose this way for my life to flow.

I am not willing to compromise,
I'm as free as my beautiful butterflies.

I continue to grow to this day and will always strive to do so. Today I discovered I have a very high empathy level, I am a poet, writer of a health action plan, artistic photographer, mentor, teacher, facilitator, avid scrapper and a great friend to those I love. Find your passion in life, your values and your mission. You can never stop growing, learning and experiencing new things. It makes you a better person.

I hope this helps you in some way. You are not crazy because of emotions going up and down, minute by minute. It doesn't matter what your crisis was – a divorce, loss of a child – any loss is difficult. I would write a happy poem one day and five or six sad ones at the same time.

I have learned that my passion is life-long learning. My values are integrity, honesty and ethics. My mission is to continue to learn, help others by mentoring, teaching and to grow through their trials and tribulations – because we all have them. If you had asked me what my passion, values and mission were, after a 22-year marriage, I could not have answered any of those questions. Today I can, because I have learned so much about myself.

I am very proud of whom I am, what I stand for, and that I am willing to share. It is just a matter of being intentional instead of reactionary. I wish all of you who read this will begin to grow, accept the ups and downs, and appreciate every time you start taking two steps forward and only one step backwards. That is the beginning. Keep moving forward, continue to grow and love yourself for the beautiful person you are becoming inside and out. Always love yourself first, because then you will find out who you really are.

Gloria is in the process of publishing her life works. The poems are a reflection of her life. She hopes that they will create healing spirits in each of you as you read them.

TRIUMPHANT
WOMEN

Jenna

Conquering the Battle of the Bulge

It's been a battle of the bulge ever since I was little. I've had tummy rolls, stretch marks and a puffy face. There are more pictures of a chubby-me than I'd like to admit to, but this has been my life. I am the oldest of three children and come from a family of big eaters and stocky, muscled frames.

Like so many women and men who grew up big, I've battled with obesity all of my life. At times I was successful only to later gain it all back in record time. Today I've made a lot of progress in my own journey, but I wouldn't consider myself a success just yet. The pursuit towards the best possible health is never really reached since it is not a static goal. But I will say I have reached a lot of success, beginning not so much when I was six, but about 20 years later.

I was 26 and had just delivered my daughter. Earlier in the year when I had found out about the pregnancy, I was panicked that I would experience the same weight-gain I had with my first child. With my daughter, I weighed in at about 240 or 250 pounds when I became pregnant and already was wearing a size 20/22.

When she was born I was so proud I didn't weigh in at 300 pounds (my goal was NOT to gain the same 50 to 60 pounds I had with her brother) and was happy for the moment at 280 pounds. Some of that weight came off after her birth, but I managed to maintain my weight at 270 pounds.

Fast forward about a year: Evie was starting to walk and we were learning that she was a very curious baby and got into everything given the chance. I had tried unsuccessfully that year to lose weight using the same methods and strategies I had used before to get some weight loss. I bought aerobics videos, borrowed tapes from my mother, watched what I ate and drank water. Yet every time I got started, I usually stopped about a week or two into it for a lot of different reasons.

Most of the time, the diet (i.e., nutrition) piece of it was never something I could ever commit myself to for the rest of my life. I LOVED junk food, especially cheeseburgers, Dr. Pepper and ice cream. Some days were better than others and I would be able to keep that little voice at bay when it beckoned me to my favorite indulgent craving, but other days I would get frustrated and decide 'to heck with it' for the moment/day and indulge.

Or the diet would fail because I hurt myself, which I think has had a lot to do with my past successes and subsequent failures. From my father I inherited what doctor's consider "high knee caps" – where the patella (knee cap) sits higher than normal. The knee joint still functions the way it should; however the ligaments and tendons are stretched and are not as strong as they should be. Especially in sedentary and overweight individuals, the muscles become even more relaxed, which resulted in my knees dislocating practically at will. In fact, before I became pregnant with Evie, I was wheelchair bound due to a fall: my knee had dislocated as I walked down the hall at work, which caused me to fall. The way that I fell caused me to break my opposite ankle in three places as well as my fingers. Since my fingers had to splinted it was unsafe for me to walk with crutches (my foot had to be casted) so I was prescribed a wheelchair for six weeks. Add to that the fact that this happened after I had been on a new job for only one month! Factor in already low self-esteem about my body and having the entire building running to my aid and finding me on my belly on the linoleum floor in a less-than-flattering position. Suffice it to say, I have had a lot of trouble staying active for fear of hurting myself.

All of this combined and contributed to my weight gain over the years until I stopped to look at myself in the morning and realized I couldn't stand what I saw looking back at me. I couldn't recognize myself anymore. Plus, my daughter was beginning to walk. I was literally scared that as curious as she was, she would run out the front door while playing and run right into the street and it would be up to me to run out and save her from a passing car. The question became, "Can I do it?"

If my daughter was in danger and it was up to me to run to save her, would I be able to do it? The answer I gave myself further disappointed me: no, I probably would not be able to do it. I was so scared that I would hurt my knees or fall and break a bone that I subconsciously believed I could not and would not run, if even to save my own life from a burning building. I hated that about myself, but I honestly believed it to be true.

I also tried to convince myself that I simply was not meant to be a healthy size and shape. At this point, I was fitting into dress sizes 26/28, depending on the cut, and was so frustrated with trying to lose the weight that I quit trying. I gave away all of my old, "skinny" clothes, and resigned myself to being a big woman.

I never liked that decision, though, and I didn't like that I was letting my weight and unfit body dictate what kind of mother I could be. A couple of months after I gave everything away, I decided again that enough was enough. I was lucky enough to work at a building that shared a parking lot with a gym and I figured I could go over my lunch break and get a little bit of a work out in and have lunch at my desk afterwards. I joined the gym and felt really empowered that this change was going to happen, I was going to MAKE it happen, once and for all.

The gym was offering a special on personal training in addition to the free session you got when you joined. I had just celebrated my 28th birthday and had convinced my family to chip in to help me afford six personal training sessions. I'm a pretty driven and determined individual and I knew – having been down this path successfully a time or two before – what the fundamentals were: eat less and move more. But I wanted the personal trainer to help me start with making working out a habit, so I arranged to see him once per week. I also drove our workouts to some degree. I had specifically asked him to spend time showing me what machines to use for my goal: to lose weight and be healthy for myself and family. I had never worked out in a gym consistently enough before to really know what machines to use, how to use them and why I should use certain piece of equipment over others. I knew I wanted to learn these things. I also wanted my trainer to focus on my technique to make sure I was exercising correctly and safely so I could continue without hurting myself so that I would want to just quit.

Within six weeks, I was looking good. I had lost about 15 to 20 pounds. My trainer couldn't give me a lot of nutrition advice (a trainer's scope of practice revolves mostly around exercise and they leave nutrition advice to the dieticians). My eating habits had improved, but were still not to the level where they needed to be. I was still eating a lot of processed foods and the meals I made at home weren't "clean." The gym had a website for members to go to for help along the journey and part of that website included a nutrition plan you could customize to fit your goals and lifestyle. The meal suggestions and recipes offered were easy and my family enjoyed them, but more important the foods were "cleaner." I began to eat foods with a smaller amount of saturated fat, fewer sugars and empty calories. Within the next three months, right before my company's holiday party, I was elated to be able to fit into a dress size 18. I hadn't been that small in almost ten years!

I let myself move on the positive momentum. I began to read different fitness magazines to get tips, be motivated and to learn more about leading an active and healthy lifestyle. My biggest motivators were being able to play with my daughter (who did eventually learn to walk and yes, she was into everything!); being able to see my body changing before my eyes, and fitting into smaller and smaller clothes (my co-workers began to give me their hand-me-downs that they either no longer wanted or could not fit into anymore), and being able to walk down a flight of stairs without any fear or pain. The latter was a really big deal to me.

Because I had grown up with two horrible knees for which the only possible solution was surgery (which I refused), stairs had slowly become a major obstacle for me. Going up wasn't usually a problem for me since I was strong enough to climb, but it was always when coming down the stairs that I ran into problems. It literally hurt me to go down stairs. Every step made my knee crunch, which I winced away as best I could. I also had a very big psychological problem when it came to stairs: I was deathly afraid of climbing down stairs and one day having my knee not bend the way it's supposed to and falling down a flight of stairs, most likely in a public place, that would leave me horribly embarrassed in more ways than one. So I typically opted for the elevator, if one was available, or I braved the stairs one step at a time, gripping the handrail as hard as I possibly could.

However, after losing more than 50 pounds, I was able to take the stairs more and more. When I could only go one step at a time I was able to gradually walk down a flight of stairs and then be able to "bounce" down stairs effortlessly. I'll never forget the day when I walked down that flight of stairs at the gym for the first time without pain or fear. That feeling was absolutely amazing, almost freeing, to me. I tried to explain that to my trainer who only stared back at me like I was the world's biggest dork for being excited about climbing down stairs, but for me it was a very big deal and when I realized I really did have what it takes to do it. It was worth his puzzled expression.

Eventually, I was able to bring my weight down under 200 pounds, which was another fantastic milestone. My family was incredibly supportive of my commitment to better health and my children became two of my biggest cheerleaders. My husband was also a major source of inspiration and motivation during this time. For him it was really nice because almost every month or two he had a new wife!

When my gym closed and my 30th birthday approached, I began to notice a plateau in my motivation. I had reached my initial goal of losing weight and getting back into a size 11 but I wasn't satisfied or motivated. In addition, our 10th wedding anniversary was coming up. I wanted to continue on my path but I wasn't sure how much. I had made a new goal a few months earlier to try to get in shape to do a bodybuilding/fitness competition but to get to that level of fitness took a lot more work that I simply wasn't sure I could do. Taking a break (for our anniversary) did a lot for me. Right before the trip, I had found a new place to work out, but there was a lot more to it than that.

The wellness center wasn't simply a gym, but a program that aligned health professionals under one roof and towards a common goal: to improve the health, well-being and lives of the patients. When I joined, I had reached a weight of about 155 and it was my goal to get to 140 to145, which had eluded me. In the program, I met first with a doctor for a physical and learned some things about myself that I didn't know, like the fact that my left leg is about a 1/8 inch shorter than my right. Interesting. From there I partnered with another personal trainer who worked with me to help strengthen my weak areas, such as my core and abdominals, and push me harder than I could push myself. In addition, I was prescribed a set of three group fitness classes (cardio, resistance and flexibility focused) and was matched with a nutritionist. And when I had an overuse injury, I was able to use the physical therapy services. The wellness center was truly the blessing I needed to find to get back on my path!

In the three month program I managed to lose a few more pounds of fat, but after training fairly consistently for a couple of years, my muscles were growing bigger and thus weighed more than my fat weight. While this is definitely good, it was still frustrating to step on the scale and not see that number I wanted. It has taken me some time to realize that it's not the number on the scale that matters. However, this is easier said than done, and there are still days that I'd like to see that number staring back at me. I guess it's just part of being an American woman, but I don't let it get me down for long. I just slip on a favorite dress and take a nice look at myself in the mirror and marvel at the accomplishments I have made in my life.

Today I'm still on my path towards health success, but my focus is beginning to shift. Going down this road, you see the impact you have on the lives of those around you and you don't realize the influence you have until it smacks you in the face. So many friends and co-workers have commented, complimented and just stared in amazement when they realize it's Jenna they are looking at and many have asked me the age-old question, "What's your secret?"

There is no secret. The answer was right there from the very first time I had to battle it: eat right, move more. The missing piece of the equation, however, is to stay with it and really make it a part of your life. This is why diets fail, because people refuse to make it a life change. It's not a life*style* so much as it's a conscious choice you must make in regards to how you are going to live your life. On this journey I have discovered my natural inclination to help others and am now a certified personal trainer and I'm teaching two of the group fitness classes at the wellness center. Currently, I teach four to six classes a week and am looking to certify in more classes in the future.

I've also learned a lot about myself. When I started out, I felt a little misdirected in life and uncertain what kind of future I wanted. By taking control over this part of my life, I've found my drive again and that I can do ANYTHING I want to in life. The choice is up to me if I am to succeed or not.

I've also learned that I am human and it's still necessary to find balance. I'm an extreme person and a lot of my behaviors have always been extreme: if I start something new that I feel very passionate about, I put 150 percent or more into it. But when I burn out, I really burn out. I'm still learning how to find a balance.

This has led me to also recognize that there are some very powerful psychological motivators towards some of these behaviors that have contributed to my obesity but thankfully doesn't separate me from the majority of American women. I honestly believe I have a slight addiction to food; I like to eat for no real reason sometimes and other times it's out of boredom or depression – or some other reason I have yet to see. When I want to eat, I think about it. And then I think some more. And some more. And continue to obsess until I indulge the craving and, consequently, over-eat, leading to guilty feelings. It is a negative downward spiral. Although I have acknowledged this pattern, I feel I have only begun to get at the root cause of my personal battle and to better understand the struggles and battles of my clients and participants in class.

To me, it's incredibly satisfying to share this story with so many others who are fighting this battle and feeling frustrated with themselves and society. I've been there; I know what it's like. I grew up as "thunder thighs" with two bad knees, a grandmother who would let my cousins and brothers have the "good" snacks and I got the fruit and calorie-free popsicles, where Christmas celebrations and birthdays always meant some well-intended but disappointing exercise video or equipment, and shopping for clothes meant paying top dollar at special shops for bigger people – and still feeling embarrassed at having to put on a shirt sized 3x.

That was my past. However, if I can come from that background and achieve what I have been able to accomplish with life, volleying all kinds of things at the same time, I know that you can do it too.

My favorite quote from Lao Tzu sums it up better than I ever will be able to: "At the center of your being you have the answer; you know who you are and you know what you want."

Don't stand in the path of your success any longer. Vow to be triumphant!

TRIUMPHANT
WOMEN

Kelly

Believe in Yourself

I was born in Santa Monica, California to Canadian parents. My father had been in the military for both Canada and the U.S. Although he had been discharged from the military by the time I was born, he ran the household like we were in the military. My mother was seen and not heard and had little to no input about what happened in the household or how to raise my brother and me. During my entire childhood, I only remember a few times when I ever heard by parents say they loved me, especially my father. As I grew older, it became more difficult. We moved a lot, not only in the same city, but from the U.S. to Canada and back and then to California and Nevada. We finally settled in Arizona, although we moved three times by the time we settled here. Needless to say, I did not make friends easily. I thought, why? We will just move again!

Wherever we lived, I was not allowed to have anyone over, at least not in the house. I could not give out our phone number and always had to take my brother with me wherever I went, which was quite frustrating and embarrassing.

In my father's eyes, I could never seem to do anything right. I longed for him to be proud of me. In school, I was an "A/B" student. One day I remember bringing home a report card with all As and my dad's response was "You can do better."

I was devastated. That was not the response I was expecting. When I was in grade school, my father got hurt and was unable to work. In order to deal with the pain, he turned to alcohol. During high school, it just got worse. I wasn't allowed to date, and couldn't participate in school activities. I had wanted to be on the track team and in the band. My father felt that high school was not for "extra curricular activities" and forbid me from participating. Although I loved my father very much, we just didn't seem to see eye-to-eye. I told him I was going to move out on my 18th birthday and planned to attend community college. He laughed and said I would never make it on my own and that women did not need a college education, they just needed to finish high school.

To my knowledge my father had not completed high school, although he was very intelligent. My mother only had a 5th grade education because she had to quit school due to the war and go to work to help support the family. I would be the first in the family to graduate from college.

I was determined to make more of myself. My parents were both blue collar workers. Dad was a mechanic by trade and my mom was a hotel housekeeper. So on my 18th birthday I asked a friend with a big truck to help me move the few things I had to a friend's house. My mom later told me she cried and it took weeks for her to get use to not looking for my car lights at night.

During my senior year of high school, I participated in a program that allowed students to work and also get school credit. After graduation I continued to work for the company. But in order to make it on my own and attend college, I had to get a second job.

When I was 20, I married the love of my life. He was four years older than I was and had just been discharged from the Army. My dad did not like the man I married and did not attend my small wedding ceremony. He also would not allow my mom to attend. My husband was not allowed in my parents' home.

When I was 21, my father died. My mom called me to tell my something was wrong. She said dad had not been feeling well. When I got to the house, I found my father. He had committed suicide. He had been sick for some time and was too proud to have people help him do daily things any longer. My parents had been married 27 years and my mom was devastated. She didn't know how to be on her own. She dealt with the loss with alcohol. It was a very devastating point in my life. It took several months for me to come to grips with it.

When I was 25, my husband and I had our first daughter. It was exciting, yet scary. I was now responsible for another human being. She was beautiful, healthy and I loved being a mom. Five years later, we had our second daughter. By now there was a lot of friction between my husband and me.

In hindsight, I seemed to have married my father. They had both been in the Army; both came from dysfunctional families and both were alcoholics. Now that I was a mom, it seemed that part of the insecurity I had felt all my life was subsiding. I loved being a mom and was involved in all the activities: Girl Scouts, gymnastics and school activities. I was apparently trying to prove to others that I could do it all. Or was I trying to prove something to myself?

And, oh yeah, I was still attending college part time and finally graduated with my bachelors. It only took me 15 years to complete, with essentially no support from my husband. He did not like the fact that I was trying to better myself and that I was away from the house a few days a week. He would have to "baby sit" his own children! I survived the next few years by doing anything I could to stay away from the home. I immersed myself in my daughters and work; I became a member of the neighborhood homeowners association, and took on a second job. My husband was not the loving, supportive father that two beautiful little girls needed to grow up confident and strong in a man's world. I was not going to have my daughters go through what I had as a child. My children were going to hear "I love you" often and receive hugs and kisses as long as they would let me give them. These were things I had not received much of when I was younger and I believe had a lot to do with my feelings of insecurity.

For five years I played with the idea of filing for divorce, but wondered how I would make it on my own. We owned a house and I had my mother living with me and my two daughters. My mother had been injured at work and was only living on Social Security. Since we needed a babysitter for the girls and she needed a place to stay, I had her move in with us. She lived with me for 15 years before she died. At work, I met a man and we became very dear friends. He was dating someone, but he was always there for me to vent to. It was with his guidance that I was able to find the strength within myself to proceed with the divorce. I wasn't sure how, but I was going to get through this and my girls would be better off without their father in their daily lives.

I finally decided to meet with the attorney to file for divorce of my husband of 18 years – my best friend since I was about 12 years old. It was the hardest thing I ever had to do. I was breaking up the family. This was my fault…or was it?

The divorce, as difficult as it was, was the first step in finally taking ownership and acceptance for things in my life. My whole life I felt that I have been told I was not good enough, was not going to make anything of my life, and I have always struggled with feelings of insecurity.

Insecurity still haunts me today, but I have learned to be more conscious of it and not let it hinder me from accomplishing something. It was after the divorce that I realized that I was being held back. Since my divorce, I have had more confidence and have been able to handle tough situations better. I have been more successful both at work and personally. At work, I have moved into a mid-level executive position with the company where I have been for 30 years and have tripled my salary. Not the typical result for a woman after a divorce. Personally, I have a wonderful boyfriend who has been a father figure to my girls. I have enjoyed traveling, both for work and with my girls, mom, and boyfriend. As challenging as it was taking care of my mom for 15 years, it was nice to have her around. The girls got to be with her, and she was a part of our everyday lives. It was a devastating loss when she passed away a few years ago. The support of my daughters and boyfriend made the loss easier, though.

My daughters have grown up to be very wonderful, intelligent and confident women and I am blessed to have them in my life. It is sad that their father, who moved out of state not long after the divorce, has not been a part of their lives for about 10 years. He has missed so much and it will be difficult for him to ever have a meaningful relationship with them. He occasionally writes to them and still harbors a lot of anger, which is unfortunate.

Life is too short and we must live it to the fullest. We should surround ourselves with people that have the same or similar morals, ethics and beliefs and who will support us and help us succeed. After years of frustration and unhappiness, I have finally accomplished that in my life. I have my beautiful daughters, my loving boyfriend and great close friends that love me and support me.

My message to all women struggling out there is to believe in you, even when others don't. Set goals, and never, ever give up on your dreams. A woman can be triumphant, strong and successful and doesn't need the approval of a man to do it.

TRIUMPHANT
WOMEN

Leanna

Dreams Do Come True

Courage – what is courage? I believe it means many things to different people. What first comes to my mind is something someone has who fights a life threatening disease or does something that frightens them. Looking back I have never thought of myself as being courageous, but being just plain stubborn and determined.

I was born in Indiana and grew up being very close to my family. We did everything together, and went on wonderful family vacations. Our family seemed to have many friends, but my parents were especially close to the Hills – mainly the Hill brothers and their families. One of the Hill brothers had already left the clan and moved to Arizona but always returned for holidays and special occasions. The ages of the Hills' children and the children in my family were very similar. My sister was the oldest, and I was the baby with ten years between us. Our two families blended together quite nicely. I always referred to the elder Hill as "Grampa Charley".

Of course, as time goes by, things change. Grampa Charley passed away, and a few months later one of the brothers died. The family seemed to dissolve around us, and when the last Hill brother moved to Arizona, we found ourselves alone.

Trying to find a new niche, we moved, also. My older sister and brother remained in northern Indiana, and the rest of us went first to southern Indiana, then on to Tennessee, and finally we found ourselves in Arizona. Once again, we were back among our old friends. I was 10 years old at this time, and I was glad to be back with my very best friend, Karen, who was so much like a sister. We shared everything.

I also became reacquainted with the Hill boys. They were okay, but we were not impressed with each other. Once settled, my mother returned to Indiana to bring back my sister, who now had two children of her own. Life to me seemed perfect. My dad had a good job, we had great friends, and I was doing very well in school. I was even on pompom.

At 16 and a senior in high school, the most devastating thing that could ever happen, happened. My father –my hero – passed away. It wasn't that I had never lost a loved one before, but this was something I thought could never happen to me. As with most little girls, my father had always been the most important man in my life. My mother took it very hard and went back to Indiana to stay with my brother. My other brother was fighting in Vietnam, so this left me with my sister. It soon became clear the arrangement wasn't going to work out, so I went to stay with Karen's family.

I was having a very hard time adjusting, but to help out I babysat Karen's little brother. One evening I was taking care of him and trying to clean up the kitchen when in came Tom Hill, a cousin I had not seen for many years. Tom's father had passed away a couple of years earlier, and we began to talk. He could understand just how I was feeling; you could say we made a connection. He was so sweet, but he was a very busy person with a complicated agenda of his own. He was in college and heavily into rodeo. Karen wanted him to date me but he was two years older and not really interested.

We kept running in to each other and it seemed like fate. One day he finally asked me out. It was the beginning of forever, and three months later he asked me to marry him. I had just turned 17, and was still in high school but all the dreams I had when my father was alive had vanished. It seemed as if it all now had a purpose. Had I not been staying with Karen, Tom would not have come back into my life.

My mother was excited – she loved Tom so much. But first I needed to graduate. A wedding date was set for June 29, 1968. Because I was only 17 and Tom was 19, both parents had to give signed approval. As we began to make all the arrangements, a wrench was thrown into our plans. Tom was drafted. Despite a soldier's pay of $98.00 a month, we were still determined to make everything work, and everything seemed to fall into place when after boot camp Tom was stationed at Ft. Huachuca, Arizona. The big day came and we said our "I dos" – of course with by-standers remarking it would never last, that we were just too young.

With a new dream at hand, we were both determined to be together, no matter what. His next duty station was at Ft. Benjamin Harrison in Indianapolis, Indiana. This would work out just fine. I could not stay with him, but I had an aunt and uncle in South Bend, and my brother was in Madison. With their permission, I could take turns staying with them.

I could help them out during the week, and Tom would join me on the weekend. It could be a win-win for all of us. This tour of duty did not last long, and Tom got his orders to go to Okinawa in November.

Again, I felt devastated. I knew I could go back to Arizona and live with my mother, who had just remarried. I really did not want to do that, but as a soldier's wife I only got $49 a month. I would have to get a job and work through it. So that was the plan. Tom went off to Okinawa and I went home to Mom.

However, this plan was not meant to be. I was home only a few days when I found out I was pregnant. I was so sick. All I wanted was to be with Tom. Now what was I going to do?

When Tom first arrived on the island he was not impressed, but figured he'd spend most of his time on base so it was not a big deal. When I told him the big news, he wanted me with him. Tom was a not a rank high enough to have his family live on base, so if I went to be with him we would have to live off base. He was not sure it was a good idea. He felt the island was the armpit of the world and he did not think I would like it. I told Tom it could not be that bad. I'd seen slums before and there was nothing so bad we could not handle it. Besides, my brother had spent many days on Okinawa and also went back and forth many times while serving in Vietnam. He loved Okinawa and even married an Okinawan girl. So how bad could it be?

The cost of living was very low and Tom had just gotten a pay raise to $130, so together we would get $179. Once the baby was born, my check would increase to $135 a month, but that was still months down the road. So together we decided I should go to Okinawa.

I began to make plans, but there were so many things that needed to be done. A plane ticket alone was several months' pay. I had to have shots, and because I was pregnant they could not be given all at once. Then there was the dreaded passport that took forever to get. Even though the morning sickness never went away, stubborn determination kicked in and the day finally came. I was going to Okinawa.

That morning I awoke and sheer terror overcame me. I had never been so far away from home without my mother at arm's length to turn to if I need her. The morning sickness was now an all day event. I was going to be all alone, with a layover in Tokyo, a foreign country where few people spoke English. I thought, "Oh my God, I must be crazy. What have I done?"

I knew I couldn't turn back. So much had been done and so many people had helped me get to this day. "Oh God, please help me," I prayed.

With everything I had in me, I boarded the plane. As the plane left the runway I had only one thought: at the end of this journey was everything I needed – Tom. My first stop would be Los Angeles (L.A.), and as the plane made its descent, I remember thinking how large the city looked.

I had only three hours to get to my next terminal, which I intended to go straight to. I did not want to miss my flight. I must have looked really pale. A business man setting next to me asked me if I was okay. I started to cry, and of course he could see I was pregnant. I told him it was my first time away from home, my first plane ride, and I had no idea where the terminal was I needed to go to. When the plane stopped and we got up, he grabbed my carry-on bag and told me to follow him, that he would help me to the tram and show me where I needed to go. The tram had a large sign with all the airlines listed and the terminals they flew in and out of. I did miss getting off the first time around but, the second time around I knew exactly where I had to go. I got to the correct gate with plenty of time. I do remember spending much of the layover in the restroom.

The next leg of the journey was from L.A. to Tokyo, with a few hours layover in Honolulu. I had envisioned this beautiful island, with a large international airport. When we landed it was raining, the wind was blowing, and it was downright cold. Since the layover did not involve changing planes, I did not feel as overwhelmed and decided to take a short walk around the airport. The entire airport had only one main entrance in and out of the terminal. Inside there was one small snack stand. I planned to get something to drink, but even a small glass of milk was $5. I felt that was outrageous and found a drinking fountain. I quickly found myself back on the plane and in my seat. Before I knew it, we were back in the air. Next stop – Tokyo.

I was a little anxious about Tokyo. I had an overnight layover and had booked a room for the night through the airline. I had no idea what it would be like. I was still having problems keeping anything down, and the food being served only made it worse so I tried to sleep as much as possible. Just as I felt sleep coming on, I heard the pilot's voice on the intercom. With much excitement he was explaining to everyone that we had just crossed the international dateline and everyone would be receiving a certificate. All I knew is that I had been in the air more than 17 hours and all I wanted to do was land and maybe get some sleep.

Then there in front of us was Tokyo. It was huge, and looked so dirty. I again felt this feeling of terror. I had to find my luggage and wondered how I was going to find my room. No one spoke English. I felt a huge lump in my throat and I was trying with all my might to hold back the tears. I turned and there stood a little Oriental man holding a small sign which read, "Mrs. Hill, please follow me."

I nodded my head at him that I was Mrs. Hill. He smiled this wonderful grin, waved his hand and started to walk away. As the sign instructed, I followed his every move. He picked up my luggage, took me through customs, loaded me on a bus, and showed me to my hotel room. Then with the only words he spoke the entire time he said, "I be back morning," and away he went.

It was a tiny room with rice paper thin walls. The bathroom was the only room with solid walls. You could see shadows and hear everything. Needless to say, I got very little sleep and was up in plenty of time and ready to go when I heard the knock on the door. The same little man with his big bright smile picked up my luggage, waved his hand again, and away we went.

He stayed with me all the way to the plane door, and still with a smile he nodded and said "have nice trip," turned, and was gone. I made my way to my seat, and when I looked around noticed this plane was much smaller then the other ones and I began feeling very uncomfortable. There were no other Americans on the plane, and the stewardesses were not speaking English. When they were finished explaining the on-board instructions, one of the stewardesses came over to me and in very broken English explained to me what they had said. When they started handing out breakfast everyone seemed so pleased, but when I saw what it was I only became nauseated and hurried off to the back of the plane.

Fish…who eats fish for breakfast? It had been two days and I had eaten very little. I did not know if I was sick because of the morning sickness or because of hunger. In my mind all I could think of was Tom and how I hurt to see him. I hoped he realized what I was going through to get to him.

The flight did not seem to go on very long when I looked out the window and saw a long narrow piece of land. It looked so small. Was this Okinawa? The plane headed straight for it. "This must be it," I told myself as my stomach started getting butter-flies.

It would not be long now. Ahead somewhere among the crowd of people was Tom. The airplane door opened, and I hurried down the steps looking everywhere. "Where is he? I don't see him."

Then, there he was, a huge smile, eyes full tears. I could not get to him fast enough. Those wonderful arms engulfed me, one of the most wonderful kisses I could ever have imagined. "I made it, I am safe," I thought to myself.

As soon as we left the airport I could see there would be a lot of things to get used to. Tom was right, and the word "slums" did not come near describing our surroundings. The sewage lay open and exposed and rats were running all over the sides of the road. I was glad to get to our little apartment Tom had found the week before. He had done a great job furnishing it and getting it ready for me. I was so proud of him.

We settled right in getting ready for the baby and learning how to live on our soldier's pay. I finally got over my morning sickness, and in June on Fathers Day the most beautiful little boy, Tommy, made his entrance into our world and nothing has been the same since.

During our stay we spent our weekends driving around the island. The island was only 65 miles long and 12 miles at its widest point. There were only two main cities, both centered on air bases. Away from the cities were beautiful little quaint villages. The longer we were there, we found ourselves drawn into their history and gained a much greater respect for all they had been through. We learned so much about its people. They were not considered Chinese or Japanese – they considered themselves as just Okinawan. Most of their traditions were closer to the Japanese. I found them to be a very proud people. Since World War II, Okinawa had been a possession of the United States. Their economy was very poor and many worked for the military for a mere 12 cents an hour. They very much wanted to be a part of Japan, which they thought would raise their standard of life.

After two years it was time to return home to Arizona. I could still not fly government, so this meant Tommy and I would have to go home on commercial planes. I left two weeks before Tom, but this time I was better prepared. Many things had changed in two years. There would be no layover in Tokyo. We had a flight to L.A. on a new kind of plane, a 747 with United Airlines. The only stop was on the small island of Guam. Since the only landing field on Guam was a military base, this leg of the flight was full of soldiers. Landing on the Guam airstrip was an adventure of its own. The strip reached from one end of the island to the other with only water on the other side. It literally took the entire strip to land and take off; it was very scary.

Very few new passengers boarded from Guam, and once in the air I realized how big this plane really was. It had two levels with a spiral staircase, and upstairs was a lounge and first class. We were on the bottom level and there could not have been more then 50 people on the entire plane. Needless to say, Tommy was allowed to play and run up and down the isle where our seats were. The seats also lay down flat, so when he finally wore himself out he had plenty of room to stretch out and go to sleep. I must admit the flight went better than expected, and the food was even good.

The only little glitch was that we ran into a storm which caused the flight to get behind schedule. I began to get very concerned, as we only had 30 minutes to change planes in L.A. and that time was being eaten up quickly. I relayed my concerns with the stewardess. I told her I had to get to Phoenix and I had to get on that plane as my entire family was waiting for us. When the plane landed, it was obvious we had missed the connection. To my surprise the stewardess came to me, helped pick up all my carry-on items which included my overnight bag, and diaper bag. I had my purse and Tommy. She then instructed me to come with her. I never moved so fast carrying a small child. All at once we were boarding a really small plane compared to the one we had just been on. This one was a business flight from L.A. to Phoenix. The pilot had relayed my plight to the passengers and they agreed to hold the plane. Looking back I realize what a big deal that was. Something like that would never happen today. I was so grateful, and as I thanked everyone with tears streaming down my face, I found our seats.

It was only an hour flight, but it seemed like forever. With the anticipation of seeing my mother my stomach was all aflutter, and Tommy was getting really fidgety. I changed his clothes into a little western one piece outfit my mother had made and sent to us for the trip. On his feet included western boots two sizes too big. He looked so cute but as always happens with a baby, just before it was time to land we had to do a diaper change. We landed, and as I was trying to pick up all my things a very nice gentleman offered to help carry my bags.

When we walked into the terminal gate, there everyone stood. With tears in our eyes and waving arms everywhere, we rushed in. Everyone had to get a hug and kiss, and all the while that nice man stood waiting to hand us the bags. Of course in the quickness of changing planes our other bags did not make it, so we had to go to the office to fill out paperwork. The airline told us they would deliver it to the house when it arrived. As I walked from the airport terminal to the car and looked over at the Phoenix skyline, an overwhelming feeling came over me. I was home. The circle was now complete.

There are so many stories that could be told, but it was this experience that was the framework for the rest of my life. I left a teenager and returned a young woman with much more confidence, and I was no longer afraid to embark on new things. I learned I was capable of getting things done on my own and taking care of others' needs as well. I was so much better prepared to handle what life might be preparing for me. However, I must admit that I still do not like to fly but will do so when it's necessary.

In 1972, we added a daughter and then we were four. Tom and I had been two spoiled kids when we married and many thought we would never last. We learned to work together as a team. "Together" is the key word, and as long as we never forget that, we can make all our dreams come true.

Now, blessed with five grandchildren, I am still on a never-ending journey with that handsome, young rodeo cowboy that I connected with in the kitchen 42 years ago. Dreams do come true!

TRIUMPHANT WOMEN

Martha

Out of the Land of Mirabah and Into the Gates of Elim

Growing up in a military family had its share of difficult experiences. Having to leave friends, school and belongings on a moment's notice could be painful and confusing, especially for the children involved. Dad always had a way of trying to re-direct our plaintive cries with his usual mantra, "Don't cry; be strong!"

After his last tour to Japan, we moved to Merced, California. A year later, he was killed by a drunk driver. I was 12 and devastated. Our mother fell apart and we were sent spiraling into lives of utter dysfunction. My older sister was 16 at the time of his death and became our surrogate mother. There were five siblings, all girls, ages 16, 12, 8, 7 and 5 years of age. And there was mother who was 32 years old, physically present but emotionally absent. She was never the same after his death. A "bitter root" took hold of her, and everyone and everything was contaminated.

I married young and found myself in an abusive relationship. I often wondered what was wrong with me. What was I doing to cause him to be so violent? What was I doing that "made him commit adultery?" Was this all there was to marriage and life? Suicide became a tempting alterative to the abject loneliness and abuse. But, I kept remembering Dad say, "Don't cry; be strong!"

At the time, divorce was not an option. My marriage was tumultuous and I wondered what effect it was having on my children. We never spoke about what was happening. I had no family support. My mother lived in Pleasanton, California and didn't want to be involved. She kept telling me what a charming, attractive and hard worker my spouse was. That I should be grateful he married me because I was a plain Jane. I was lucky that my children were beautiful thanks to him.

Yes, he was very attractive and hardworking. Actually, he lived for his job. He was also the tall, dark and handsome type. If you told him that the moon was beautiful and yellow, he could convince you that it was green and ugly. At first glance, he was also quiet and unassuming. Yet, I felt like I was living on the edge of a volcano. I felt so alone and too embarrassed to call my sisters. They had their own lives and lived far away. Everyone believed my spouse was the ideal spouse. No one knew about the seething rage below the surface. I was the perfect mate for this dysfunctional relationship. I was a doormat. I was willing to compromise to keep the peace until…

For years, my only friend was my next-door neighbor, Nell. Nell was a retired pediatric nurse and an angel. I confided in her only after she came over one day, after hearing screams from the night before. She asked me about the bruises and I broke down crying. I felt ashamed and could hardly speak. She put her arms around me and prayed. I was terrified. She told me I deserved better and to call the police. The next time it happened I did call the police but they did nothing except tell me to calm down or I would be arrested. It was the 70s and domestic violence was a well-kept secret. He kept telling the policemen that I was crazy and they believed him. My children believed him, too. Pretty soon I began to believe that I was crazy. Self-doubt set into my very bones.

Then one day, while at the local health clinic, I practically stumbled into the "Free Mental Health Counseling Office." The sign in the window said, "Do you need help? Free counseling."

Frightened I stepped into the small office. An attractive, well-dressed woman sat at the only desk in sight. I could hardly get the words out of my mouth, but managed to ask, "Can you help me change? I don't know why I make my husband hit me."

Tears began to roll down my face, as I turned away from my two youngest boys napping in their stroller. Choking I continued to blurt out, "Could I make an appointment with the counselor? Can someone help me stop making my husband so mad?"

She smiled and told me she was the counselor. That was the beginning of a dangerous and compelling road toward freedom. The counselor would call or come to the house to check on the kids and me. At one of our last secret meetings she told me that I had three choices to make. She believed that I would be killed, maimed or go insane. I was dumfounded and in denial. She came to the house to meet my spouse and to offer help. But he told her it was my problem and he was fine and that I was delusional and the cause of any problems we had. Later she told me she made her assessment and felt that my spouse had a narcissistic personality with borderline sociopathic tendencies. She told me things would only escalate and that I shouldn't have to compromise my beliefs or needs to placate him and keep the peace. She told us that we both needed ongoing counseling. He declined and I was too afraid to pursue any more sessions. He left the house furious and I never saw her again.

I was afraid and had nowhere to go. I began looking for a way out. I had tried to stay with family in Modesto and Pleasanton, California, but after a few weeks, he would find me and drag me back. Sometimes, I returned willingly. This cycle went on for years. Things would be okay for a few months then it would start all over again. I went to speak to our priest and he told me I would go to hell if I got a divorce. I was horrified and terrified.

What could I do? I was already in hell. I felt like a hostage. I walked around as if I were in a daze. My head hurt, my body hurt, I hurt all of the time. As long as I didn't ask questions or ask him to help out with the kids or house, had dinner made and the house clean, and said nothing about or to his interfering mother, we got along just fine. My poor children were like zombies, oblivious to our circumstances. Or so I thought. I tried to hide as much as I could from them but, as they got older, they began to identify with him. During one of our fights they told me to shut up so he wouldn't get mad. "Stop being a bitch, mom," they shouted.

I was crushed. He had just gotten a subpoena for a paternity test. How much more could I endure? I pleaded with God to intervene. With no answers in sight, the anger began to build. I suppressed my feelings and began to get physically ill. Then my anger toward him began to spill in front of the children as rage about his infidelities and behavior. They hated me for speaking ill of him. That was my greatest regret. At one point he agreed and we went to church with an aunt and uncle who had just become "born again." We both gave it a good try, but the wedge between us grew bigger.

I got a divorce in 1975, became homeless, and I eventually had to send my children to live with my sister and her husband. I got a job with the phone company and put in for a transfer to the Bay area to be with my kids.

Being away from my kids and the waiting was agonizing. I suffered what the doctor called a "minor breakdown." After six months, the transfer never came and I reconciled with my ex. The abuse cycle continued for another four years, until I was able to make the final break. Reality finally jogged me into action when he pointed a rifle at me in front of our younger two boys, then 10 and 12 years of age. They helped me wrestle the rifle from him and they ran to the neighbors and called the police.

Desperation and fear set in big time. The rules had changed. Now, he was actually planning to kill me. How could I get away alive? How could I support my children and keep them with me? I had no work skills or life skills and he refused to pay child support. Every time we separated and after the divorce even the local Child Support Office couldn't locate him. My children were just as afraid as I was. During the last four years of our relationship, he kept taking the children from me. Each and every time he reminded me that I couldn't make it without him and that I was a failure.

I felt like a failure because I was only able to get menial jobs and was evicted from almost every place the children and I lived. He would come and take the children without my consent and without legal rights. But he didn't care about legalities. The last time he showed up and took them, I had just been offered a promising entry-level position with the state as a file clerk. After years of prayer, I would finally have been able to feed, shelter, clothe and keep my kids.

When I got home, the boys were waiting by his car and packed. I cried out, "What are you doing?"

They told me they were going to go live with their dad because I couldn't support them and they felt like a burden. I couldn't believe what they were saying. "Don't go," I cried as they got into the car without kissing me or hearing about my new job.

Afraid of what my ex-spouse would do if I ran after the car; I crouched down sobbing like a coward in pain. My daughter, who was 18 at the time and pregnant, tried to console me as we watched them drive away. That night I attempted suicide by swallowing a handful of Valium. My daughter and a widow neighbor-friend kept me awake by plying me with black coffee and walking me up and down and all around the apartment. The next morning I felt like I had been hit by a train. I cried all weekend. I finally realized that I had to pull myself together and start all over again. I was about to become a grandmother for the first time.

Every day I asked myself "why?" Why was there no help available? Why did my prayers go unanswered? Then one day shortly after starting my job with the state, I found some pamphlets in the lobby about domestic abuse. I felt a sort of apprehension as I began to read them. Finally, I began to understanding my circumstances. Maybe, just maybe, I wasn't a failure after all. Maybe I wasn't crazy.

I called their hotline. I cried and asked questions and they listened. Eventually, I found and got counseling. I had read once that "self-knowledge was the beginning of wisdom." The information I was trying to process slowly was sinking in but I kept trying to justify staying alive. One night after praying for some relief, I began to remember a memory of tip-toeing into my children's room and kissing their foreheads as they slept when they were babies. I could even recall the way they smelled: clean, sweet and powdery. How could I leave them behind? Hurting them was never an option. They were for me my blessings, my loves – they were everything to me.

Then one morning, as I lay awake waiting for the alarm to sound, a cool breeze floated gently though my open bedroom window carrying the sweet, ceaseless chirping of the sparrows nesting in the tree outside my window, and I felt a quickening within me. It was memories – blessed memories of my grandparents kneeling in prayer at dawn, and a feeling of being safe and surrounded by love. Scriptures began to flow through my heart and mind like joyful music. Slowly I began to process the information I received about domestic violence. I now had hope and a plan of action.

Courage and relief came gradually. I regularly attended counseling and began to read and read. Each day began and ended with Psalms, especially Psalms 23 to 27. Then Isaiah 54 ending with Jeremiah 29:11, and the domestic violence plan. Eventually, I returned to church and slowly the healing process began. Being separated from my children was excruciating. But, I knew I had to keep going. I had to find a way to get well, get them back and to survive. The fog that I had lived in for so long began to lift.

I enrolled in college and after 20 years of struggling, I eventually graduated with a degree in Behavioral Science. In 2001 my ex-husband came to see me at work. The war was over. He had recently reconciled with his second wife and had gotten counseling. We didn't speak again until July 2005. He asked me to pray for him because he was sick and dying. He wanted to make sure our kids did not cry when he passed on.

I prayed for him but told him the children would cry for him because they loved him and would miss him. He died of liver cancer on November 23, 2005. I was alone in my apartment when our oldest son called to let me know that his father had passed on. I wept inconsolably.

Overcoming had been a slow process for me, but the things I learned about myself and my ex-spouse brought forgiveness, understanding, and the blessed assurance that, "I can do all things through Christ which strengthens me."

God had always been with me, my deceased father's spirit and words –"trust God"– were with me as were Nana's and Tata's strong Christian faith during the worst of hardships. Their enduring love was with me, along with the scriptures that had taken root when I was a child. I am so very thankful for everyone whose encouragement, professionalism and humor played roles in God's plan for my life. Finally, the valuable information and counseling I received from the domestic violence hotline and the counselors had all fallen into place as I stepped "Out of the Land of Mirabah and into the Gates of Elim."

TRIUMPHANT WOMEN

Patricia

Too Ashamed to Tell

What do I do next? At the age of 25, I stood in the living room of my unloved home and wondered where I would go. I couldn't go back home; that's why I got married. I couldn't stay in the marriage because it was tearing me down. The mental abuse had taken its toll on me and my self-esteem was in the toilet. But I played the part of being happily married and having it all together because I couldn't let anyone know my secret. I had made the biggest mistake of my life marrying a man I did not love, but marrying him had been my ticket out of my dysfunctional childhood.

Looking back at that time, I should have had great confidence. I was pretty, tall, smart, and the perfect size 10. For years I had men treat me like I was a piece of meat and any disgusting act they wanted to expose me to, they did. It started with my stepfather. At first I didn't tell because my mother was always hollering and I didn't want to be blamed, but when I did tell, I was shocked at her response. Nothing.

There was no outburst of disgust or defense of her poor, powerless daughter. She asked him if he did it and he violently denied it. Even though it was both my sisters and me telling the stories, she still believed him and took his side. In the years following, I became too ashamed to tell anything.

I didn't like boys much in my teenage years. I don't know if it was because of the fear of my mother's wrath or most boys always wanting only "one thing" – I just wasn't interested. My mother preached you couldn't study two Bs (books and boys), so to keep her off my back I did extremely well in school and studied books. I decided that going to college was going to be my way out.

To my surprise, my mom would not allow me to go away to school. She said she didn't have the money to support me. Instead, I went to a local college where I received a partial scholarship but I had to pay out of pocket for the other expenses. To keep my dreams alive, I went to school during the day and worked the night shift at a department store.

I met my ex-husband on the job. When he and his co-worker tried to make small talk, I just ignored them. But he was kind of cute with a beard, and was very tall. Weeks of him pursuing me finally landed him a date. Now, I was scared out of my wits to tell my mom I had a date; surely it should be okay because I was going to college now.

We dated for seven months before we got married – not because the passion and love was so strong, but because I was pregnant. Yeah, I made it all the way through high school and my first year in college before I gave in to the pressure of having sex. What made it even worse was that I got pregnant the first time I had sex and it hadn't been anything like I'd seen in the movies. I could have avoided getting pregnant because a friend was trying to get me to go to Planned Parenthood with her to get birth control pills, but I refused because I was afraid that someone would find out.

Being married was nothing like I saw on TV either; it was more like what I grew up in – dysfunctional. We lived in a three-family bungalow on the west side of Detroit. I went to school and he supposedly went to work. I found out later after he lost his job that he would leave for work, but either left early or never arrived. Things went from bad to worse and over the years things never got better. I needed some help and the only one I knew I could call on with no strings attached was Jesus.

When I was growing up we always went to church. My mother "sent" us to church. It was a storefront church three blocks from our home. The pastor was really into the youth and we got to participate a lot. To be honest, the majority of the congregation was youth. We were at church all day on Sundays. After the morning service, the first lady would prepare dinner and we would have dinner at the pastor's house. She made the best macaroni and cheese.

At a minimum, one Sunday per month the pastor preached on the prodigal son. As a child I wondered why he preached the same sermon every month. I didn't know at the time it would be the sermon I would hold onto to get me through life. I remembered the prodigal son was ashamed, too, but he came to his senses and his father received him with open arms. The revelation hit me: Jesus loves me and he died on the cross for my sins and I didn't have to be ashamed. He would receive me back just like I was. I knew I couldn't waste what he did for me on the cross, and I decided to go back to church.

Going back to church was hard at first because I had to deal with the ridicule at home, but I needed God's help. I started going to church with an older lady at my job. She was a true Christian – sweet, kind, compassionate and never had a cross word to say about anyone. The more I went to church, the stronger and determined I became in not wasting my life. I decided if God would take me back, I would never leave him again. I had more than me to think about. I had a child.

The word of God was just the spark I needed to get my fire started. As I sat under the Word, I began to hope again and my hope turned to faith. I listened to sermons, read the bible, and prayed daily. I no longer saw myself as defeated with nowhere to go, but I realized I could make the decisions I needed to help my daughter and myself out of the situation we were in. Suddenly, I had the courage to face any challenge that came my way.

My favorite scripture is Psalms 34:8, "Oh taste and see that the Lord is good; blessed is the man that trusted in him."

The more I trusted his word and applied it to my life, the better things got. It wasn't overnight but God proved that he was bigger than any problem or obstacle. I got jobs that I didn't have the qualifications for and was successful at them. I had bosses that understood the importance of being a good mom and I would get time off with pay to attend a parent/teacher's conference or whatever I needed to do for my child. I have had some ups and downs, but overall, the good outweighed the bad and each day I rejoice because the love of God keeps me in perfect peace, even in the middle of the storms that blow through my life.

TRIUMPHANT
WOMEN

Shauna

The Journey Through the Pain and Back Again

It has been seven years since my mother passed away. She fought the battle with esophageal cancer for two years, which had progressed into lung cancer in a matter of months. I watched her go from being a very vibrant person into a small lifeless shell. From the time that she found out that she had cancer, it was two years and five months before she was gone. One week after her 65th birthday she went to be with the Lord. My two sisters and I were at her bedside with her. I leaned over and said "'I love you, Momma," and she replied, "I love you too, baby."

She took her last breath after she said that.

A year after my mother passed away, I noticed that my husband's right lymph node just under his ear was swollen. He had told me that he had a molar that had been bothering him for a few months and that he was just putting up with the pain. A few months passed by and I watched the lump in his neck get bigger. I told my husband that I was going to make an appointment with the dentist for him. The tooth was definitely infected and was subsequently pulled. My husband was given some antibiotics for a month to get rid of the infection. He followed up with his dentist the following month. The swelling had gone down a little but not very much. The dentist advised my husband to see his doctor to find out why the swelling was not subsiding. Since the toothache was no longer bothering him, my husband put it off. Two more months came and went when I noticed another lump, the size of a walnut, under the first one. I told him he really needed to go to the doctor and have it checked out. He told me that it wasn't bothering him and that he would let me know if it hurt. He seemed angry that I was concerned for him. Two weeks later he came home from work and said, "Make me a doctor's appointment."

The following week, we were in the doctor's office. The doctor checked him over and immediately referred us to an ENT (ear, nose and throat) specialist. We were told to set up an appointment as soon as possible. A week later we were at the ENT doctor. The doctor threaded a scope through my husband's nostril and down his throat. The doctor took some biopsies. The biopsies came back positive and my husband was informed that he had cancer at the base of his tongue and was immediately scheduled for surgery to remove the cancer.

The days leading up to the surgery were hard for me. We were at the same doctor's office that I had taken my mother to just two years prior. A sad, scared nauseated feeling came over me every time I entered the doctor's office. I kept thinking to myself that if I had only gotten my husband to the doctor earlier and not let him wait, that things would have or could have been different.

Two weeks later we were in the hospital for the surgery. By the time the surgery was finished, the doctor had removed two lymph nodes, part of the base of his tongue, all of the muscle mass on the right side of his neck (from right under the ear to his clavicle bone), and also removed his jugular vein on the right side. After the surgery, the doctor came out and told me that the surgery had gone very well and that there was still a small spot on the tongue. My husband would have to go through 11 weeks of chemotherapy and 35 radiation treatments.

The months that followed were very hard. Chemo and radiation were taking their toll on my husband. He lost 85 pounds and looked like a walking skeleton. My husband was finding it harder and harder to go through his radiation treatments. During the treatments, he had to put on a plastic mask (made specifically for him and which restricted any movement) and then was strapped to the table. Once on the table, he had to lie perfectly still for 45 minutes while the radiation burned through his neck. The blistering on his neck was pretty bad. I had to step up and help him get through this torture. Every time he stepped into the radiation room, I would hold his hand and say a prayer. During this time, I was still working full time – on a four, three, three day alternative schedule. I worked twelve and a half hour shifts – some weeks four days and other weeks three days. My mother-in-law and father-in-law came to help out with taking my husband to his appointments on the weeks that I couldn't.

I felt hurt and jealous that I couldn't be the one to take him all of the time. I was afraid of losing my husband and I wanted to spend every moment with him. There were all kinds of emotions running through me. But mostly, I think it was anger. I was angry that no one from church had returned my calls. Angry that my husband was sick. Angry that my in-laws were doing something that I felt I should be doing. I was just angry at the whole world. I was mentally and physically drained.

In order to keep everything together, I took a new position at work as a lead supervisor and I was kept very busy. Between my husband and my job, I was feeling worn down and tired. It was getting harder for me to get up in the morning to go to work. One day while visiting my sister, I told her how tired I was feeling and she told me that she had some over-the-counter diet pills that gave her energy. She gave me some to try out. I tried them and they seemed to give me energy. Little did I know that they had phen-phen in them and that they were very addictive. I started to take them more frequently and eased right into an addiction to them.

A year had gone by and my husband was able to have his feeding tube removed. He was able to eat again by mouth but he could only have liquids. Everything he ate had to be liquefied in the blender first. He returned to work with the same company that he had been working for when he got sick. He had been with the company for 10 years before he found out about the cancer. A special position was made available to him. It was a desk job that he was able to get up from every couple of hours so that he could eat (he was supposed to eat every three hours). As the months went by, he was able to eat more food, and eat less frequently. He started to get his freedom back. This newfound freedom, though, seemed to exclude me. We were both working for the company and making good money. Through this phase of our marriage, my drug addiction got worse and my husband started gambling. No matter how much money we were making, we started fighting over money and him being gone all of the time. We couldn't make enough money to keep up with our addictions. Finally, I decided that I could not continue living like this – I had had enough! I had to get away from this madness.

It had been three years since I had been to church and I missed the fellowship with other Christians. I knew that I could not clean up my act where I was. The drug abuse was all around me – at work, with friends, even with my sister. Subsequently, I quit my job, cashed in my 401(k) and bought a plane ticket to go and stay with my son who lived 3,000 miles away. I was starting over.

At the time, though, I did not realize how much "starting over" I was about to do. I did a lot of soul-searching while I was staying with my son and his family. I started going to church with them and was actually reading the bible again. I started feeling better and felt I was back on track.

Six weeks after I left my husband, I received a phone call that our vehicle was going to be repossessed. Since I couldn't pay for it from my son's house, I called my husband and asked him to pay the bill. I knew that I had enough in the bank to get it caught up. My husband simply said, "No, they can take it."

We only had one more year to pay on it. I begged him but he kept telling me that he was not going to do it. Little did I know that all the money in the bank was gone. My husband and his sister had gambled it away. I was crushed.

That weekend I returned home. I knew it was bad but I had to deal with it. The arguing over money continued and the bills were not getting paid. Three months later, we were locked out of the house and on the streets. We were staying with whoever would let us at the time. I finally talked my other son into letting us put up a tent in his backyard. He already had a house full with our daughter and three girls living there. We lived out of that tent for a little over a year. Then my daughter and granddaughters moved into their own place and we moved into the house.

I didn't know it at the time, but God had a plan for us. When we shut him out of our lives and did things our own way, down we went. Throughout this journey, God has both humbled and shown his mercy to both my husband and me. Only when we brought God back into our lives, did we find peace and love again – for only with God are all things possible. Today, God has brought my husband and me closer than we have ever been in our 27 years of marriage. We didn't realize it at the time, but God has been with us throughout our journey.

It has been seven years since my mother passed away and it has been a long hard road without her. I know that God has been with me through it all. Today we are still living with my son and my husband is back to work. I stay at home and take care of the family. We are slowly getting back on our feet again. It hasn't been easy and we know it will be a few more years before we can pay back all the debts. I know in my heart, though, that God truly has a plan for each and every one of us. We just need to listen and we will all triumph.

TRIUMPHANT
WOMEN

Vernita

My Journey to Love

Everyone was saying that I shouldn't marry Yasin. My friends were telling me, my parents had said don't go to Afghanistan. But somehow I knew it was the right thing to do. After all, I was in love.

Yasin and I met on the street at Ohio State University when he stopped me for directions. It took me three months before I finally agreed to go on a date with him. But we quickly became friends. He lived only two doors down from my rooming house. We often walked to school together and met for lunch at the automat on campus. He was a junior in engineering and I was a freshman in education. We took a lot of walks, either along the river or down High Street. Yasin didn't have any money. He was on full scholarship and the living allowance wasn't much. I worked to pay my expenses. So mostly we walked and talked. Sometimes we went to a small local Chinese restaurant for special occasions. We didn't talk of marriage, but just enjoyed our friendship.

Yasin graduated. It was time for him to go home to Afghanistan. It was a sad time for both of us. He was a young man from Afghanistan and I was from a small farming community in southern Ohio. I had never traveled outside the United States. But somehow our friendship became a great bond. Even though we were from opposite ends of the earth, our morals, our beliefs and our outlook on life were the same. My family was extremely conservative. Even though my parents had met Yasin, and I think liked him, they did show strong opposition for me getting strongly romantically attached to him.

Yasin wrote me a letter on his way back to Afghanistan. He mailed a letter from Germany asking if I would marry him. I could not answer. How could I? He was travelling. When he arrived in Kabul he sent me a telegram again asking if I would marry him. I immediately sent a reply telegram that I would be there on February 19th. I had to allow at least two weeks to get my passport and tickets, and to give my notice to the university where I worked.

So on February 15, 1967, I flew from Columbus, Ohio, to New York with my airline ticket to Kabul, Afghanistan, a $20.00 bill and a handful of change (mostly pennies). I had gotten rid of my few belongings and packed a blue skirt, a blue sweater, a red blouse, an orange dress, and my blue suede Hush Puppies. I also put in my small blue suitcase a small red carpet. I wore my blue dress and my red shoes, and my blue wool coat. I had to carry my mandolin since it didn't fit in the suitcase. I also carried a small book to read on the way. I was 20 years old and was going to Kabul to get married.

While spending a couple of hours at the airport in New York, I wrote a postcard to my parents informing them of my journey. Even though I had told them that I was going to Afghanistan, I was sure that they didn't think I would really go.

When I was called to board my flight on Air France to Paris, I was excited. Here I was actually traveling to another country. I made sure that I got a seat next to a window. I didn't want to miss a thing. It may sound funny, but I kept my eyes glued to the window watching the ocean below until it got dark.

We arrived in Paris early in the morning. When I went to claim my suitcase, it wasn't there. My luggage (yes, my one suitcase) was lost. When I complained that my suitcase was not there, an airport employee asked me to follow her.

We arrived at the top of a long wide staircase. She motioned for me to go down. As I descended the stairs, I saw what I would describe as a sea of suitcases. The whole floor was covered with all types of luggage. The employee asked me if I saw my own suitcase. I responded that I did. There it was, my small blue suitcase. She told me to pick it out and take it. I could have taken any one of the hundreds, maybe thousands, of bags. But, as I have always been an honest person, I grabbed my own suitcase by the handle and went back up the stairs. No one checked if I was getting the correct bag. In fact, the employee left me as soon as I said that I saw my bag.

I had about four hours to wait until my next flight. To pass the time, I walked around the airport and looked at the exquisite shops. There were shops selling perfume, lovely French fashions, and souvenirs. Having still more time, I went and bought myself a chocolate bar and found a comfortable chair next to a bright window where I sat and enjoyed eating my candy and reading my book.

My next flight was to Greece. I remember flying in that afternoon to Athens and seeing the bright sun reflecting off the many whitewashed houses on the hillsides. There was such a beautiful contrast of the white houses, the dark blue tiles on the roofs and the turquoise sea below. I had only a little over one hour before getting my next flight, so I found a way to a roof at the terminal and stood overlooking the city of Athens. It was beautiful! I stayed there the whole time admiring the scenery.

I pulled myself away from the mesmerizing scene just in time for me to arrive at the gate for my flight to Istanbul. This was a short flight. And I had a short wait at the airport as well. I think I had less than an hour's wait. Here they also had enticing shops, But, I didn't want to buy anything. I wanted to keep my $20 bill. I was getting my meals on the airplanes, so I didn't have to buy food anywhere. And, soon I would be on my way to Teheran.

I knew that I would be spending the night in Teheran. When I received my airline tickets in Columbus, a letter was enclosed stating that since there was no flight to Afghanistan until morning a room would be reserved for me and was paid by Iran Air.

A car was waiting for me at the Teheran Airport. The driver introduced himself in a cordial manner and drove me to a small, but clean hotel. I arrived at the hotel around 8:30 p.m. I was tired but still excited about all the new places and people I was experiencing.

As I got out of the car, the driver left me standing in front of the hotel. The inside was dimly lit and outside was completely dark. I went inside to the registration desk. A middle aged man stood up when he saw me and asked my name. He gave me a smile and asked if I would follow him up the stairs. As he was escorting me to my room, he asked if I would like some dinner. Since I didn't know if I would have to pay for the dinner, I declined. I thanked the man and went inside the small clean room, where I sat on the edge of the bed all night. I was afraid to lie down. I thought I might fall asleep and not be able to get up in time to leave the hotel at 5:00 in the morning when the car was supposed to return to take me back to the airport. I patiently waited all night. Fortunately, there was a clock in the room, so I was able to know what the local time was. I was able to come down the stairs of the hotel on time where the car was waiting for me, and left for the airport.

Iran Air was great. The breakfast was very good. The people were friendly. But one thing bothered me. The airplane had piped in music. Only one song played: Frank Sinatra's "Strangers in the Night". I have nothing against Frank Sinatra; in fact, I like his singing and his songs. But to hear the same song over and over for a few hours is close to torture. Even today when I hear that song, as I smile to myself, I don't know if I am cringing or laughing.

We were to arrive in Kabul around 8:30 that morning. I was excited and busy looking out the window of the airplane. I must not have heard the first announcement. But I noticed that the ground was brown. I was expecting white snow on the ground. Finally, I heard why. We were landing in Kandahar. Kabul Airport was snowed in. A blizzard had covered Kabul during the night.

We landed in Kandahar. The airport terminal was a very large, brand new building of ultra modern design, and was empty. The walls were mainly glass. As I looked out all I could see was desert. No other buildings were visible. The airplane on which I arrived was the only airplane in sight. As I entered the airport, no other people were around other than the passengers and crew. Someone who must have been an airport employee herded all the passengers into a large room. Except for the passengers, the room was completely empty – it held no furniture or any employees of the airport. The terminal had a modern P.A. system so a voice overhead announced that since the airplane could not land in Kabul, we had the following choices: return with the airplane to Teheran, find alternative transportation, or join the bus going to Kabul at 3:00 p.m. I immediately knew that I was not going back to Teheran. I had to get to Kabul. So I chose to wait for the bus.

Most of the passengers got back on the airplane to return to Teheran. I stayed standing in the large room. I was alone. Someone came in the room carrying my suitcase. Evidently, he was an airport worker that I had not seen. He smiled at me as he put the suitcase next to me. He returned after a few minutes with a chair. He placed the chair next to me and motioned for me to sit. I did, and he left the room.

I waited for some time. It was hard to say whether it was an hour or many.

The young man, who brought my suitcase and chair, came over to me. He asked in simple English if I would like something to eat. I did feel hungry. I probably had been waiting longer than I realized. So I looked up at him and said, "Yes."

I didn't think anything about money. He began to walk away from me and motioned for me to follow him across the huge room. I abandoned my suitcase and chair. I didn't even think about anyone taking my luggage. No one else was there.

I followed the young man to a beautifully clean kitchen. There was a spotless stainless steel counter with stools around it. Behind the counter was a beautiful shiny grill (it looked brand new). The young man went behind the counter. I sat on a stool. He prepared for me a ground meat patty (an Afghan style type of hamburger) with some local bread. He placed the plate in front of me and smiled. I smiled back and began eating my delicious lunch. The young man disappeared while I was eating. When I finished I still didn't see him. So I got down off the stool and returned to my seat in the other room.

Again I was alone for a while. Finally, a man and a woman entered the room. They walked over to me and introduced themselves. They were a couple from Canada working with the United Nations. The young Afghan man again miraculously appeared with two chairs and carried them over for the couple. The room was so large that when the couple sat about ten yards away from me it still looked close. We were close enough to carry on a conversation. They asked me what I was doing in Afghanistan. I replied that I had come to get married. They looked puzzled. I must have looked very young to them. They were probably in their 40s. Just when they were about to ask something else they were interrupted. From the far end of the room an Afghan entered through the side door. He was tall, and wore typical brown Afghan style clothing and a dark brown turban. He had a light brown shawl wrapped around him and carried a rifle over his shoulder.

The Canadian woman looked at him and then over at me and asked, "Aren't you afraid of him?" I replied that I was not. Evidently the Afghan was using the airport terminal as a shortcut because he exited the other side of the room as quickly as he had entered. The Canadians didn't talk with me the rest of the afternoon. The three of us just sat and waited.

Around 3:00 p.m. there was another announcement over the P.A. It was surreal to hear a public announcement overhead when only three people were at the terminal. The voice, from wherever it came from, announced the arrival of the bus. The young man came into the room and showed us the way out of the terminal and led us over to a worn out bus. In fact, I couldn't tell if it was an old bus or a makeshift bus created from an old truck. It had seats and windows, although some of the windows were broken. I climbed in with my suitcase and mandolin. I went all the way to the back seat and spread my belongings along side of me. The Canadian couple followed but sat two seats in front of me. We waited for about fifteen minutes until three Afghan men leaped into the bus and sat in the front seats. We were the only passengers except for the driver and his young assistant of about 12 years of age. During our trip it was the boy's job to jump out and put a wood block behind the wheel for a brake and remove it when we started up again.

After traveling for a few hours it became dark. The driver often sang, sometimes at the top of his lungs. Around what I thought to be ten o'clock that evening we arrived at the town of Ghazni. The driver took us up a hill where there was a two story building. A man came out all wrapped up in a blanket. The ground was covered with snow. He and the driver exchanged words for a few minutes. The driver returned to the bus and started up again. The Canadian couple turned around and explained to me that the driver thought the inn would provide us with some food. But the inn keeper said that it was too late and that he didn't have anything. So we had to leave.

It was strange. I never thought of food, although I ate when the opportunity afforded me. I never thought of sleeping except when I had a chance, but mostly I stayed awake for these three days (or was it four?) as I was afraid of missing my connections.

The driver continued on with his passengers toward Kabul. It was late and extremely dark, except for the silver shine of the snow. There must have been about three feet of snow on the ground. The bus had no heat. Fortunately my coat was warm and I curled up in that back seat looking out at the sky. It was amazing. There were so many stars! I don't remember seeing the moon, but the stars were so plentiful that the sky gave the appearance of a black ceiling covered in sparkling diamonds.

I don't really know if I fell asleep or not. The driver kept on singing at the top of his lungs. No one complained. I think the passengers felt secure in the fact that he was happy and awake. There were no other lights that appeared other than the stars. Sometime in the middle of the night I saw a faint light in the far distance. I couldn't tell for sure, but I thought that it might be an electric light. As time went on and we drove toward Kabul, the light became more visible. I began to think that the light must be coming from somewhere in Kabul.

The bus came to a stop. I sat up straight and saw in the dim light of the night that we were at a crossroads. I also saw a jeep and a person standing next to the jeep. The bus driver got up and went down the steps. After a couple of minutes, he came back in and walked over to the Canadian couple who had fallen asleep. He woke them up. They both stood up and reached for their bags. The woman turned around and looked at me sitting in the back. She waited a minute and then walked over to me. She asked if I would like to join them. They were going to the U.N. Hostel and I could stay there. I thought for a minute. I did not have any address for Yasin. The only thing that I knew for sure was that his brother worked at the Electric Company. If I would get off in town, I wouldn't know where to go and would be roaming the streets until I found the Electric Company. So I decided that it probably would be a good thing to go with the Canadian couple. I didn't know how to contact Yasin. His family didn't have a telephone. I decided I could figure this out in the morning and then go to look for him.

The jeep brought us to the U.N. Hostel probably around 2:00 a.m. A middle-aged woman, most likely of European descent, escorted me up to a room on the second floor. It was a small room with a bed and a dresser. There was a window with the curtains closed. And there was a kerosene heater in the middle of the room. The room was very warm. In fact, it was too warm for me. I was very tired and really wanted to sleep. I hadn't eaten anything since the airport in Kandahar. I tried to turn down the heat, but was unsuccessful.

I started to feel queasy. I began to think that maybe the heater could be giving off fumes. I opened the curtains and tried to open the window. It was either locked or jammed. I couldn't pull the window up. I began to feel faint. I got down on my knees and crawled to the door. I barely was able to open the door and crawl out into the hallway. I crawled a little further close to the top of the staircase. There was no one around and it was completely quiet. I sat there on the floor all night leaning against the wall.

Daylight was just starting to stream through the hallway when a young Afghan boy of about sixteen leaped up the stairs. He saw me sitting on the floor. He looked at me, smiled, and said good morning. I smiled back and also said good morning. He left me sitting in the hallway but quickly came back within a minute or two along with a chair. He motioned to me to sit. I did and thanked him. He asked if I would like to have breakfast. I knew that I was hungry and said yes. He left again. Within a few minutes he returned with a table and placed it in front of me at the top of the stairs. Then he again returned carrying a tray of Afghan bread, hot tea, and something that he called an eggroll. It was like a crepe filled with ground meat and potatoes. And, boy, did it taste good!

I was sitting and eating my well-appreciated breakfast in the hallway when I heard a familiar voice. I couldn't see clearly down the stairs, but I knew the distance wasn't far. I called out, "Yasin?"

He called back up, "Vernita, is that you?" I immediately stood up and ran down the stairs. There was Yasin. Somehow he had found me!

Postscript

Many people think that it was quite risky for young woman to travel alone around the world during a time when there was very little communication, and transportation wasn't easy. There is also the fact that I had only $20. I have often been asked me through the years, "Why did you do it? Weren't you scared?"

I always tell them that I was in love. I knew no fear. I knew Yasin couldn't get back to me so I had to get to Yasin. Yasin and I have had a wonderful life together. And, after 42 years of marriage, two children, and four grandchildren, I definitely think the trip was worth it.

Editor's note:

*Vernita is the author of the award winning novel, **The Quest for the All Seeing Eye**. This historical adventure novel covers many of the traditions and culture of Afghanistan and is available through Amazon.com and/or can be ordered through a bookstore. Vernita is currently writing another book about the many wonderful adventures that she experienced while living in Afghanistan for ten years. Even though at this time the book is untitled, the working title is **My Life in Afghanistan**. Look forward to it being published sometime in 2010.*

TRIUMPHANT
WOMEN

Your Name Goes Here

It is Your Turn!

We hope that these triumphant stories have inspired you to tell your Story of Courage. We have provided you with pages at the back of this book for you to get started. Once you have composed your story, we would like to encourage you to post your story at our website – *www.triumphantwomen.com* or contact us to help you. Your story could inspire millions of women around the world to become Triumphant Women! Enjoy the journey!

_____

_____

_____

_____

_____

_____

_____

_____

_____

_____

_____

_____

_____

Breinigsville, PA USA
03 March 2010
233527BV00001B/4/P